Both by calling and conviction Father Brown knew better than most of us, that every man is dignified when he is dead. But even he felt a pang of incongruity when he was knocked up at daybreak and told that Sir Aaron Armstrong had been murdered. There was something absurd and unseemly about secret violence in connection with so entirely entertaining and popular a figure. For Sir Aaron Armstrong was entertaining to the point of being comic; and popular in such a manner as to be almost legendary. It was like hearing that Sunny Jim had hanged himself; or that Mr. Pickwick had died in Hanwell.

THE THREE TOOLS OF DEATH

G.K. Chesterton

first published in

1911

For though Sir Aaron was a philanthropist, and thus dealt with the darker side of our society, he prided himself on dealing with it in the brightest possible style. His political and social speeches were cataracts of anecdotes and "loud laughter"; his bodily health was of a bursting sort; his ethics were all optimism; and he dealt with the Drink problem (his favourite topic) with that immortal or even monotonous gaiety which is so often a mark of the prosperous total abstainer.

The established story of his conversion was familiar on the more puritanic platforms and pulpits, how he had been, when only a boy, drawn away from Scotch theology to Scotch whisky, and how he had risen out of both and become (as he modestly put it) what he was. Yet his wide white beard, cherubic face, and sparkling spectacles, at the numberless dinners and congresses where they appeared, made it hard to believe,

somehow, that
he had ever been
anything so morbid
as either a dram-
drinker or a Calvinist.
He was, one felt, the
most seriously merry
of all the sons of
men.

He had lived on
the rural skirt of
Hampstead in a
handsome house,
high but not broad, a
modern and prosaic

tower. The narrowest of its narrow sides overhung the steep green bank of a railway, and was shaken by passing trains. Sir Aaron Armstrong, as he boisterously explained, had no nerves. But if the train had often given a shock to the house, that morning the tables were turned, and it was the house that gave a shock to the train.

The engine slowed down and stopped just beyond that point where an angle of the house impinged upon the sharp slope of turf. The arrest of most mechanical things must be slow; but the living cause of this had been very rapid. A man clad completely in black, even (it was remembered) to the dreadful detail of black gloves, appeared on the ridge above the engine, and waved his black hands like some sable windmill. This in itself would hardly have stopped even a lingering train. But there came out of him a cry which was talked of afterwards as something utterly unnatural and new. It was one of those shouts that are horridly distinct even when we cannot hear what is shouted. The word in this case was "Murder!"

But the engine-driver swears he would have pulled up just the same if he had heard only the dreadful and definite accent and not the word.

The train once arrested, the most superficial stare could take in many features of the tragedy. The man in black on the green bank was Sir Aaron Armstrong's man-servant Magnus. The baronet in his optimism had often laughed at the black gloves of this dismal attendant; but no one was likely to laugh at him just now.

So soon as an inquirer or two had stepped off the line and across the smoky hedge, they saw, rolled down almost to the bottom of the bank, the body of an old man in a yellow dressing-gown with a very vivid scarlet lining. A scrap of rope seemed caught about his leg, entangled presumably in a struggle. There was a smear or so of blood, though very little; but the body was bent or broken into a posture impossible to any living thing. It was Sir Aaron Armstrong. A few more bewildered moments brought out a big fair-bearded man, whom some travellers could salute as the dead man's secretary, Patrick Royce, once well known in Bohemian society and even famous in the Bohemian arts. In a manner more vague, but even more convincing, he echoed the agony of the servant. By the time the third figure of that household, Alice Armstrong, daughter of the dead man, had come already tottering and waving into the garden, the engine-driver had put a stop to his stoppage. The whistle had blown and the train had panted on to get help from the next station.

Father Brown had been thus rapidly summoned at the request of Patrick Royce, the

big ex-Bohemian
secretary. Royce
was an Irishman by
birth; and that casual
kind of Catholic that
never remembers
his religion until he
is really in a hole.
But Royce's request
might have been less
promptly complied
with if one of the
official detectives
had not been a friend
and admirer of the
unofficial Flambeau;

and it was impossible to be a friend of Flambeau without hearing numberless stories about Father Brown. Hence, while the young detective (whose name was Merton) led the little priest across the fields to the railway, their talk was more confidential than could be expected between two total strangers.

"As far as I can see," said Mr. Merton candidly, "there is no sense to be made of it at all. There is nobody one can suspect. Magnus is a solemn old fool; far too much of a fool to be an assassin. Royce has been the baronet's best friend for years; and his daughter undoubtedly adored him. Besides, it's all too absurd.

Who would kill such a cheery old chap as Armstrong? Who could dip his hands in the gore of an after-dinner speaker? It would be like killing Father Christmas."

"Yes, it was a cheery house," assented Father Brown. "It was a cheery house while he was alive. Do you think it will be cheery now he is dead?"

Merton started a little and regarded his companion with an enlivened eye. "Now he is dead?" he repeated.

"Yes," continued the priest stolidly, "he was cheerful. But did he communicate his cheerfulness? Frankly, was anyone else in the house cheerful but he?"

A window in Merton's

mind let in that strange light of surprise in which we see for the first time things we have known all along. He had often been to the Armstrongs', on little police jobs of the philanthropist; and, now he came to think of it, it was in itself a depressing house. The rooms were very high and very cold; the decoration mean and provincial; the draughty corridors were lit by electricity that was bleaker than moonlight. And though the old man's scarlet face and silver beard had blazed like a bonfire in each room or passage in turn, it did not leave any warmth behind it. Doubtless this spectral discomfort in the place was partly due to the very vitality and exuberance of its owner; he needed no stoves or lamps, he would say, but carried his own warmth with him. But when Merton recalled the other inmates, he was compelled to confess that they also were as shadows of their lord. The moody man-servant, with his monstrous black gloves, was almost a nightmare; Royce, the secretary, was solid enough, a big bull of a man, in tweeds, with a short beard; but the straw-coloured beard was startlingly salted with grey like the tweeds, and the broad forehead was barred with premature wrinkles. He was good-natured enough also, but it was a sad sort of

good-nature, almost
a heart-broken sort—
he had the general
air of being some
sort of failure in life.
As for Armstrong's
daughter, it was
almost incredible
that she was his
daughter; she was so
pallid in colour and
sensitive in outline.
She was graceful, but
there was a quiver
in the very shape
of her that was

like the lines of an aspen. Merton had sometimes wondered if she had learnt to quail at the crash of the passing trains.

"You see," said Father Brown, blinking modestly, "I'm not sure that the Armstrong cheerfulness is so very cheerful—for other people. You say that nobody could kill such a happy old man, but I'm not sure; ne nos inducas in tentationem. If ever I murdered somebody," he added quite simply, "I dare say it might be an Optimist."

"Why?" cried Merton amused. "Do you think people dislike cheerfulness?"

"People like frequent laughter," answered

Father Brown, "but I don't think they like a permanent smile. Cheerfulness without humour is a very trying thing."

They walked some way in silence along the windy grassy bank by the rail, and just as they came under the far-flung shadow of the tall Armstrong house, Father Brown said suddenly, like a man throwing away a troublesome thought rather than offering it seriously: "Of course, drink is neither good nor bad in itself. But I can't help sometimes feeling that men like Armstrong want an occasional glass of wine to sadden them."

Merton's official superior, a grizzled

and capable detective named Gilder, was standing on the green bank waiting for the coroner, talking to Patrick Royce, whose big shoulders and bristly beard and hair towered above him. This was the more noticeable because Royce walked always with a sort of powerful stoop, and seemed to be going about his small clerical and domestic duties in a heavy and humbled style, like a buffalo drawing a go-cart.

He raised his head with unusual pleasure at the sight of the priest, and took him a few paces apart. Meanwhile Merton was addressing the older detective respectfully indeed, but not without a certain boyish impatience.

"Well, Mr. Gilder, have you got much farther with the mystery?"

"There is no mystery," replied Gilder, as he looked under dreamy eyelids at the rooks.

"Well, there is for me, at any rate," said

Merton, smiling.

"It is simple enough, my boy," observed the senior investigator, stroking his grey, pointed beard. "Three minutes after you'd gone for Mr. Royce's parson the whole thing came out. You know that pasty-faced servant in the black gloves who stopped the train?"

"I should know him anywhere. Somehow he rather gave me the creeps."

"Well," drawled Gilder, "when the train had gone on again, that man had gone too. Rather a cool criminal, don't you think, to escape by the very train that went off for the police?"

"You're pretty sure, I suppose," remarked the young man, "that he really did kill his master?"

"Yes, my son, I'm pretty sure," replied Gilder drily, "for the trifling reason that he has gone off with twenty thousand pounds in papers that were in his master's desk. No, the only thing worth calling a difficulty is how he killed him. The skull seems broken as with some big weapon, but there's no weapon at all lying about, and the murderer would have found it awkward to carry it away, unless the weapon was too small to be noticed."

"Perhaps the weapon was too big to be noticed," said the

priest, with an odd little giggle.

Gilder looked round at this wild remark, and rather sternly asked Brown what he meant.

"Silly way of putting it, I know," said Father Brown apologetically. "Sounds like a fairy tale. But poor Armstrong was killed with a giant's club, a great green club, too big to be seen, and which we call the earth. He was broken against this green bank we are standing on."

"How do you mean?" asked the detective quickly.

Father Brown turned his moon face up to the narrow facade of the house and blinked hopelessly up. Following his eyes, they saw that right at the top of this otherwise blind back quarter of the building, an attic window stood open.

"Don't you see," he explained, pointing a little awkwardly like a child, "he was thrown down from there?"

Gilder frowningly scrutinised the window, and then

said: "Well, it is certainly possible. But I don't see why you are so sure about it."

Brown opened his grey eyes wide. "Why," he said, "there's a bit of rope round the dead man's leg. Don't you see that other bit of rope up there caught at the corner of the window?"

At that height the thing looked like the faintest particle of dust or hair, but the shrewd old investigator was satisfied. "You're quite right, sir," he said to Father Brown; "that is certainly one to you."

Almost as he spoke a special train with one carriage took the curve of the line on their left, and, stopping, disgorged another group of policemen, in whose midst was the hangdog visage of Magnus, the absconded servant.

"By Jove! they've got him," cried Gilder, and stepped forward with quite a new alertness.

"Have you got the money!" he cried to

the first policeman.

The man looked him in the face with a rather curious expression and said: "No." Then he added: "At least, not here."

"Which is the inspector, please?" asked the man called Magnus.

When he spoke everyone instantly understood how this

voice had stopped
a train. He was a
dull-looking man
with flat black hair, a
colourless face, and
a faint suggestion of
the East in the level
slits in his eyes and
mouth. His blood and
name, indeed, had
remained dubious,
ever since Sir Aaron
had "rescued" him
from a waitership in
a London restaurant,
and (as some said)

from more infamous things. But his voice was as vivid as his face was dead. Whether through exactitude in a foreign language, or in deference to his master (who had been somewhat deaf), Magnus's tones had a peculiarly ringing and piercing quality, and the whole group quite jumped when he spoke.

"I always knew this would happen," he said aloud with brazen blandness. "My poor old master made game of me for wearing black; but I always said I should be ready for his funeral."

And he made a momentary movement with his two dark-gloved hands.

"Sergeant," said Inspector Gilder, eyeing the black hands with wrath, "aren't you putting the bracelets on this fellow; he looks pretty dangerous."

"Well, sir," said the sergeant, with the same odd look of wonder, "I don't know that we can."

"What do you mean?" asked the other

sharply. "Haven't you arrested him?"

A faint scorn widened the slit-like mouth, and the whistle of an approaching train seemed oddly to echo the mockery.

"We arrested him," replied the sergeant gravely, "just as he was coming out of the police station at Highgate, where he had deposited all his master's money in the care of Inspector Robinson."

Gilder looked at the man-servant in utter amazement. "Why on earth did you do that?" he asked of Magnus.

"To keep it safe from the criminal, of course," replied that person placidly.

"Surely," said Gilder,

"Sir Aaron's money might have been safely left with Sir Aaron's family."

The tail of his sentence was drowned in the roar of the train as it went rocking and clanking; but through all the hell of noises to which that unhappy house was periodically subject, they could hear the syllables of Magnus's answer, in all their bell-like distinctness: "I have no reason to feel confidence in Sir Aaron's family."

All the motionless men had the ghostly sensation of the presence of some new person; and Merton was scarcely surprised when he looked up and saw the pale face of Armstrong's daughter over Father Brown's shoulder. She was still young and beautiful in a silvery style, but her hair was of so dusty and hueless a brown that in some shadows it seemed to have turned totally grey.

"Be careful what you say," said Royce gruffly, "you'll frighten Miss

Armstrong."

"I hope so," said the man with the clear voice.

As the woman winced and everyone else wondered, he went on: "I am somewhat used to Miss Armstrong's tremors. I have seen her trembling off and on for years. And some said she was shaking with cold and some she was shaking with fear, but I know she was shaking with hate and wicked anger—fiends that have had their feast this morning. She would have been away by now with her lover and all the money but for me. Ever since my poor old master prevented her from marrying that tipsy blackguard—"

"Stop," said Gilder very sternly. "We have nothing to do with your family fancies or suspicions. Unless you have some practical evidence, your mere opinions—"

"Oh! I'll give you practical evidence," cut in Magnus, in his hacking accent. "You'll have to subpoena me, Mr.

Inspector, and I shall have to tell the truth. And the truth is this: An instant after the old man was pitched bleeding out of the window, I ran into the attic, and found his daughter swooning on the floor with a red dagger still in her hand. Allow me to hand that also to the proper authorities." He took from his tail-pocket a long horn-hilted knife with a red smear on it, and handed it politely to the sergeant. Then he stood back again, and his slits of eyes almost faded from his face in one fat Chinese sneer.

Merton felt an almost bodily sickness at the sight of him; and he muttered to Gilder: "Surely you would take Miss Armstrong's word against his?"

Father Brown suddenly lifted a face so absurdly fresh that it looked somehow as if he had just washed it. "Yes," he said, radiating innocence, "but is Miss Armstrong's word against his?"

The girl uttered a startled, singular

little cry; everyone looked at her. Her figure was rigid as if paralysed; only her face within its frame of faint brown hair was alive with an appalling surprise. She stood like one of a sudden lassooed and throttled.

"This man," said Mr. Gilder gravely, "actually says that you were found grasping a knife, insensible, after the murder."

"He says the truth," answered Alice.

The next fact of which they were conscious was that Patrick Royce strode with his great stooping head into their ring and uttered the singular words: "Well, if I've got to go, I'll have a bit of pleasure first."

His huge shoulder heaved and he sent an iron fist smash into Magnus's bland Mongolian visage, laying him on the lawn as flat as a starfish. Two or three of the police instantly put their hands on Royce; but to the rest it seemed as if all reason had broken up and the universe were turning into a brainless harlequinade.

"None of that, Mr. Royce," Gilder had called out authoritatively. "I shall arrest you for assault."

"No, you won't," answered the secretary in a voice like an iron gong, "you will arrest me for murder."

Gilder threw an alarmed glance at the man knocked down; but since that outraged person was already sitting up and wiping a little blood off a substantially uninjured face, he only said shortly: "What do you mean?"

"It is quite true, as this fellow says," explained Royce, "that Miss Armstrong fainted with a knife in her hand. But she had not snatched the knife to attack her father, but to defend him."

"To defend him," repeated Gilder gravely. "Against whom?"

"Against me," answered the secretary.

Alice looked at him

with a complex and baffling face; then she said in a low voice: "After it all, I am still glad you are brave."

"Come upstairs," said Patrick Royce heavily, "and I will show you the whole cursed thing."

The attic, which was the secretary's private place (and rather a small cell for so large a hermit), had indeed all the vestiges of a violent drama. Near the centre of the floor lay a large revolver as if flung away; nearer to the left was rolled a whisky bottle, open but not quite empty. The cloth of the little table lay dragged and trampled, and a length of cord, like that found on the corpse, was cast wildly across the windowsill. Two vases were smashed on the mantelpiece and one on the carpet.

"I was drunk," said Royce; and this simplicity in the prematurely battered man somehow had the pathos of the first sin of a baby.

"You all know about me," he continued

huskily; "everybody knows how my story began, and it may as well end like that too. I was called a clever man once, and might have been a happy one; Armstrong saved the remains of a brain and body from the taverns, and was always kind to me in his own way, poor fellow! Only he wouldn't let me marry Alice here; and it will always be said that he was right enough. Well, you can form your own conclusions, and you won't want me to go into details. That is my whisky bottle half emptied in the corner; that is my revolver quite emptied on the carpet. It was the rope from my box that was found on the corpse, and it was from my window the corpse was thrown. You need not set detectives to grub up my tragedy; it is a common enough weed in this world. I give myself to the gallows; and, by God, that is enough!"

At a sufficiently delicate sign, the police gathered round

the large man to lead him away; but their unobtrusiveness was somewhat staggered by the remarkable appearance of Father Brown, who was on his hands and knees on the carpet in the doorway, as if engaged in some kind of undignified prayers. Being a person utterly insensible to the social figure he cut, he remained in this posture, but turned a bright round face up at the company, presenting the appearance of a quadruped with a very comic human head.

"I say," he said good-naturedly, "this really won't do at all, you know. At the beginning you said we'd found no weapon. But now we're finding too many; there's the knife to stab, and the rope to strangle, and the pistol to shoot; and after all he broke his neck by falling out of a window! It won't do. It's not economical." And he shook his head at the ground as a horse does grazing.

Inspector Gilder

had opened his mouth with serious intentions, but before he could speak the grotesque figure on the floor had gone on quite volubly.

"And now three quite impossible things. First, these holes in the carpet, where the six bullets have gone in. Why on earth should anybody fire at the carpet?

A drunken man lets fly at his enemy's head, the thing that's grinning at him. He doesn't pick a quarrel with his feet, or lay siege to his slippers. And then there's the rope"—and having done with the carpet the speaker lifted his hands and put them in his pocket, but continued unaffectedly on his knees—"in what conceivable intoxication would anybody try to put a rope round a man's neck and finally put it round his leg? Royce, anyhow, was not so drunk as that, or he would be sleeping like a log by now. And, plainest of all, the whisky bottle. You suggest a dipsomaniac fought for the whisky bottle, and then having won, rolled it away in a corner, spilling one half and leaving the other. That is the very last thing a dipsomaniac would do."

He scrambled awkwardly to his feet, and said to the self-accused murderer in tones of limpid penitence: "I'm awfully sorry, my dear sir, but your tale is really rubbish."

"Sir," said Alice Armstrong in a low tone to the priest, "can I speak to you alone for a moment?"

This request forced the communicative cleric out of the gangway, and before he could speak in the next room, the girl was talking with strange incisiveness.

"You are a clever man," she said, "and you are trying to save Patrick, I know. But it's no use. The core of all this is black, and the more things you find out the more there will be against the miserable man I love."

"Why?" asked Brown, looking at her steadily.

"Because," she answered equally steadily, "I saw him commit the crime myself."

"Ah!" said the unmoved Brown, "and what did he do?"

"I was in this room next to them," she explained; "both doors were closed, but I suddenly heard a voice, such as I had never heard on earth, roaring 'Hell, hell, hell,' again and again, and then the two doors shook with the first explosion of the revolver. Thrice again the thing banged before I got the two doors open and found the room full of smoke; but the pistol was smoking in my poor, mad Patrick's hand; and I saw him fire the last murderous volley with my own eyes. Then he leapt on my father, who was clinging in terror to the window-sill, and, grappling, tried to strangle him with the rope, which he threw over his head, but which slipped over his struggling shoulders to his feet. Then it tightened round one leg and Patrick dragged him along like a maniac.

I snatched a knife from the mat, and, rushing between them, managed to cut the rope before I fainted."

"I see," said Father Brown, with the same wooden civility. "Thank you."

As the girl collapsed under her memories, the priest passed stiffly into the next room, where he found

Gilder and Merton alone with Patrick Royce, who sat in a chair, handcuffed. There he said to the Inspector submissively:

"Might I say a word to the prisoner in your presence; and might he take off those funny cuffs for a minute?"

"He is a very powerful man,"

said Merton in an undertone. "Why do you want them taken off?"

"Why, I thought," replied the priest humbly, "that perhaps I might have the very great honour of shaking hands with him."

Both detectives stared, and Father Brown added: "Won't you tell them about it, sir?"

The man on the chair shook his tousled head, and the priest turned impatiently.

"Then I will," he said. "Private lives are more important than public reputations. I am going to save the living, and let the dead bury their dead."

He went to the fatal

window, and blinked
out of it as he went
on talking.

"I told you that
in this case there
were too many
weapons and only
one death. I tell
you now that they
were not weapons,
and were not used
to cause death. All
those grisly tools,
the noose, the
bloody knife, the

exploding pistol, were instruments of a curious mercy. They were not used to kill Sir Aaron, but to save him."

"To save him!" repeated Gilder. "And from what?"

"From himself," said Father Brown. "He was a suicidal maniac."

"What?" cried

Merton in an incredulous tone. "And the Religion of Cheerfulness—"

"It is a cruel religion," said the priest, looking out of the window. "Why couldn't they let him weep a little, like his fathers before him? His plans stiffened, his views grew cold; behind that merry mask was the empty

mind of the atheist.
At last, to keep up
his hilarious public
level, he fell back on
that dram-drinking
he had abandoned
long ago. But there
is this horror about
alcoholism in a
sincere teetotaler:
that he pictures
and expects that
psychological
inferno from which
he has warned
others. It leapt upon

poor Armstrong
prematurely, and
by this morning he
was in such a case
that he sat here and
cried he was in hell,
in so crazy a voice
that his daughter
did not know it. He
was mad for death,
and with the monkey
tricks of the mad
he had scattered
round him death
in many shapes—a
running noose and

his friend's revolver and a knife. Royce entered accidentally and acted in a flash. He flung the knife on the mat behind him, snatched up the revolver, and having no time to unload it, emptied it shot after shot all over the floor. The suicide saw a fourth shape of death, and made a dash for the window. The rescuer did the

only thing he could—
ran after him with
the rope and tried to
tie him hand and foot.
Then it was that the
unlucky girl ran in,
and misunderstanding
the struggle, strove
to slash her father
free. At first she
only slashed poor
Royce's knuckles,
from which has come
all the little blood
in this affair. But, of
course, you noticed

that he left blood, but no wound, on that servant's face? Only before the poor woman swooned, she did hack her father loose, so that he went crashing through that window into eternity."

There was a long stillness slowly broken by the metallic noises of Gilder unlocking the handcuffs of Patrick Royce, to whom he said: "I think I should have told the truth, sir. You and the young lady are worth more than Armstrong's obituary notices."

"Confound Armstrong's notices," cried Royce roughly. "Don't you see it was because she mustn't know?"

"Mustn't know what?" asked Merton.

"Why, that she killed her father, you fool!" roared the other. "He'd have been alive now but for her. It might craze her to know that."

"No, I don't think it would," remarked Father Brown, as he picked up his hat. "I rather think I should tell her. Even the most murderous blunders don't poison life like sins; anyhow, I think you may both be the happier now. I've got to go back to the Deaf School."

As he went out on to the gusty grass an acquaintance from Highgate stopped him and said:

"The Coroner has arrived. The inquiry is just going to begin."

"I've got to get back to the Deaf School," said Father Brown. "I'm sorry I can't stop for the inquiry."

THE END

ABOUT THE AUTHOR

G.K. Chesteron was an English writer, poet, philosopher, journalist, orator, lay theologian, biographer, and critic. He wrote around 80 books, several hundred poems, some 200 short stories, 4000 essays, and several plays. He had a tendency to forget where he was supposed to be going and miss the train that was supposed to take him there. It is reported that on several occasions he sent a telegram to his wife Frances from some distant (and incorrect) location, writing such things as "Am in Market Harborough. Where ought I to be?" to which she would reply, "Home".

WHAT WE'RE ABOUT

I started making Super Large Print books for my grandma. I wanted books that she could keep reading as her glaucoma and macular degeneration advanced. So I chose a font originally designed for people with dyslexia, because the letters are bold and easy to distinguish. It is set at 30 pt, nearly twice the size of traditional Large Print books.

Digital reading was too frustrating for my grandma. It could never offer the pleasures she had always associated with reading: the peacefulness of turning a page, the satisfaction in knowing a story has "this much left," and the comforting memories of adventure, companionship, and revelation she felt when seeing the cover of her favorite book. Part of what makes reading so relaxing and grounding is the tactile experience. I hope these books can bring joy to those who want to keep reading and to those who've never had the pleasure of curling up with a page turner.

Please let me know if these books are helpful to you and if you have any requests for new titles. To leave feedback and to see the complete and constantly updating catalog, please visit:

superlargeprint.com

MORE BOOKS AT:

superlargeprint.com

KEEP ON READING!

This book is set in a font designed by Abelardo Gonzalez called OpenDyslexic

ISBN 9781086236309

Printed in Great Britain
by Amazon

63349656R00068